POWER CODERS

THE BEST-SELLING APP

ADAM FURGANG

ILLUSTRATED BY JOEL GENNARI

PowerKiDS press™

New York

Published in 2021 by The Rosen Publishing Group, Inc.
29 East 21st Street, New York, NY 10010

First Edition

Illustrator: Joel Gennari
Interior Layout: Tanya Dellaccio
Editorial Director: Greg Roza
Colorist: SirGryphon
Coding Consultant: Caleb Stone

Library of Congress Cataloging-in-Publication Data
Names: Furgang, Adam, author. | Gennari, Joel, illustrator.
Title: The best-selling app / Adam Furgang ; illustrated by Joel Gennari.
Description: New York : PowerKids Press, [2021] | Series: Power coders |
Includes index. | Summary: After his Young Entrepreneur's Club meeting,
Peter excitedly tells Naya, Grace, and Tommy several ideas he has and
presses the Power Coders to help him invent a killer app.
Identifiers: LCCN 2019038964 | ISBN 9781725307681 (paperback) | ISBN
9781725307704 (library binding) | ISBN 9781725307711 (ebook) | ISBN
9781725307698 Subjects: LCSH: Graphic novels. | CYAC: Graphic novels. |
Application software–Fiction. | Computer programming–Fiction.
Classification: LCC PZ7.7.F86 Be 2020 | DDC 741.5/973–dc23
LC record available at https://lccn.loc.gov/2019038964

Manufactured in the United States of America

CPSIA Compliance Information: Batch CSPK20. For Further Information contact Rosen Publishing, New York, New York at 1-800-237-9932.

JGRAPHIC
POWER CODERS

CONTENTS

Pb 12/21/

LATER...

SHE INVENTED YOGA-YOGURT BECAUSE SHE LOVES TO DO YOGA EXERCISES AND SHE ALSO LOVES YOGURT.

AND NOW SHE HAS THIS HUGE EMPIRE, WITH AN APP THAT'S ABOUT TO LAUNCH.

SHE'S--

WE GET IT... SHE'S RICH.

AND NOW YOU WANT TO START A COMPANY AND MAKE MONEY.

FOR SURE.

WHAT ABOUT A 3-D PRINTING COMPANY THAT USES RECYCLED PLASTICS?

WE COULD CALL IT THREE-CYCLE.

OR SELF-COOLING T-SHIRTS?

WE COULD CALL THE COMPANY COOL-T.

MY FIRST IDEAS OF PETER'S CUPCAKE AND GAMING PAVILION OR PETER'S ARTISAN CUPCAKE-FLAVORED ICED TEA PROBABLY AREN'T THE GREATEST.

WHAT ABOUT A MOBILE GAME CALLED COTTON-CANDY-STORM-POCALYPSE?

WHERE YOU COULD WIN REAL CANDY?

OR MAYBE NOT.

WE NEED TIME TO BRAINSTORM SOME BETTER IDEAS.

I LIKE THE IDEA OF US STARTING A BUSINESS, BUT I DON'T THINK IT SHOULD FOCUS ON THE MONEY.

IT SHOULD BE ABOUT THE CHALLENGE OF US COMING UP WITH SOMETHING IMPORTANT AND USEFUL.

NOT GOOD.

MY BROTHER EVAN JUST REMINDED ME.

I'M HELPING HIM CLEAN POOLS ALL SUMMER.

THAT'S RIGHT.

I'LL BE BUSY WORKING AT MY DAD'S MUSEUM THREE DAYS A WEEK ALL SUMMER.

AND IT'S ALWAYS THREE DIFFERENT DAYS.

OOPS. I FORGOT TO MENTION THAT I GOT A SUMMER JOB AT PRETZEL PALACE.

MY SCHEDULE WILL BE DIFFERENT EVERY WEEK.

WELL, THERE'S MY JOB AT HUEY'S GOOEY CUPCAKES.

AND I VOLUNTEERED TO TUTOR KIDS IN SUMMER SCHOOL MATH CLASS.

HOW WILL WE EVER FIND TIME TO WORK ON CREATING A BUSINESS AND A KILLER APP?

DON'T GET DISCOURAGED.

I'M SURE YOU'LL THINK OF SOMETHING.

YOU STILL HAVE THREE WEEKS UNTIL SUMMER BREAK.

YOU CAN ACCOMPLISH A LOT IN THAT TIME.

MS. BOYD. HI!

I'M PETER.

I WAS AT THE ENTREPRENEURS CLUB MEETING THE OTHER DAY, AND I WAS VERY INSPIRED BY YOUR STORY AND YOGA-YOGURT.

THANK YOU.

IT'S NICE TO MEET YOU, PETER.

MY FRIENDS AND I HAVE THIS CLUB, THE POWER CODERS.

AND WE'RE TRYING TO THINK OF A GREAT IDEA FOR A BUSINESS OF OUR OWN.

BUT WE'RE ALL BUSY WORKING THIS SUMMER AND IT'S GOING TO BE TOUGH TO FIND TIME TO HANG OUT.

AND WITH NO FREE TIME, WE WON'T BE ABLE TO COME UP WITH A GREAT IDEA FOR A BUSINESS OR A GREAT APP, LET ALONE START ONE.

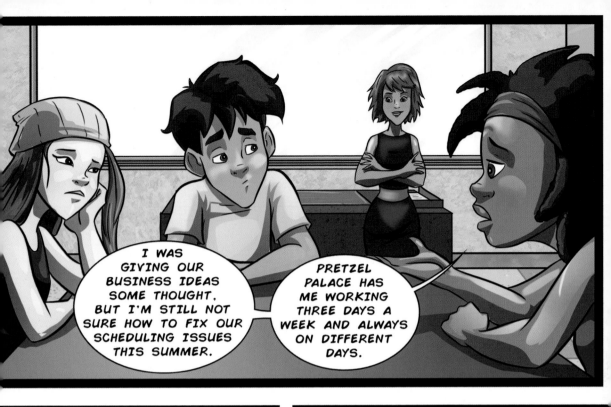

I WAS GIVING OUR BUSINESS IDEAS SOME THOUGHT, BUT I'M STILL NOT SURE HOW TO FIX OUR SCHEDULING ISSUES THIS SUMMER.

PRETZEL PALACE HAS ME WORKING THREE DAYS A WEEK AND ALWAYS ON DIFFERENT DAYS.

SAME.

I ASKED MY DAD IF I COULD HAVE A STEADIER WORK SCHEDULE AT THE MUSEUM THIS SUMMER, BUT HE SAID IT'S TOUGH BECAUSE OF RENOVATIONS IN JULY AND AUGUST.

EVAN WAS NO HELP, EITHER.

APPARENTLY POOL CLEANING IS A VERY UNPREDICTABLE BUSINESS.

I'LL ONLY KNOW MY SCHEDULE A FEW DAYS IN ADVANCE EACH WEEK.

11

HEY, CODERS!

I RAN INTO ALEXIS BOYD AT HUEY'S YESTERDAY.

I EXPLAINED HOW WE WANT TO START A BUSINESS, BUT WE'RE HAVING TROUBLE FINDING FREE TIME TO WORK TOGETHER THIS SUMMER.

SHE'S A GENIUS!

SHE HAD THIS GREAT IDEA THAT OUR SCHEDULING PROBLEM IS ALSO THE SOLUTION TO OUR PROBLEM.

WE HAVE A SCHEDULING PROBLEM THIS SUMMER.

BUT WE COULD WORK TO CREATE A SCHEDULING APP THAT'LL ALLOW US TO FIND FREE TIME WHEN WE CAN MEET UP.

IT COULD BE BOTH OUR NEW BUSINESS AND AN APP PROJECT.

I EVEN CAME UP WITH A KILLER NAME FOR THE APP.

SCHEDULE-SYNC.

COOL, HUH?

THAT'S COOL!

BUT HOW CAN WE CREATE THIS APP TOGETHER IF WE'LL ALL BE WORKING THIS SUMMER WITH DIFFERENT SCHEDULES?

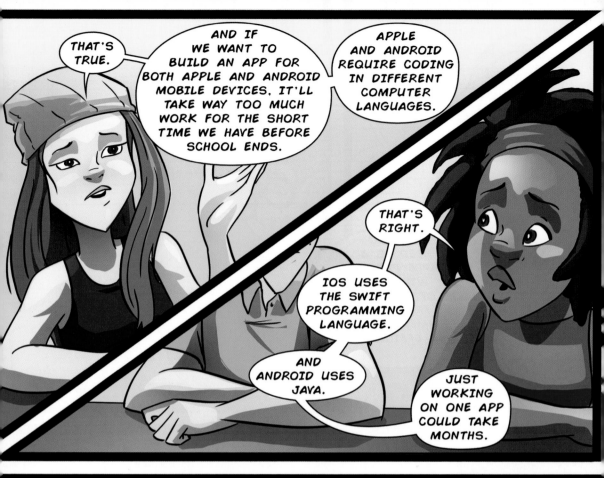

THEN, WHEN I'M NOT CLEANING POOLS, I CAN FIND SOME TIME TO HANG WITH ALL OF YOU.

I HOPE!

YOU MIGHT NOT ALWAYS FIND TIME TO GET TOGETHER, BUT IT SHOULD MAKE MEETING SIMPLER.

THE PROGRAM DOESN'T NEED TO BE FANCY. OR PRETTY.

IT DOESN'T NEED TO BE PRETTY TO START...

BUT I CAN BEGIN WORKING ON SOME DESIGNS AND LOGOS ANYWAY.

WE CAN ALL SPLIT THE WORK AND HAVE A SIMPLE WEB VERSION OF SCHEDULE-SYNC READY BEFORE SCHOOL ENDS.

LET'S MEET AGAIN AT LUNCH.

LUNCH

WE'LL NEED TO BREAK UP THE WORK FOR SCHEDULE-SYNC IF WE WANT TO GET IT WORKING BEFORE SCHOOL ENDS.

WE NEED TO DECIDE WHO WILL DO WHAT.

WE BASICALLY NEED A GRID DESIGN THAT CAN BE USED TO ENTER OUR NAMES, THE DATES, AND WHEN WE'LL HAVE FREE TIME.

IT'LL NEED TO BE HOSTED ONLINE SOMEWHERE SO WE CAN ALL ACCESS IT AND UPDATE OUR SCHEDULES.

I CAN GET STARTED ON A SITE MAP TEMPLATE.

JUST SOMETHING THAT WILL SHOW THE FEW PAGES WE'LL LIKELY NEED TO START.

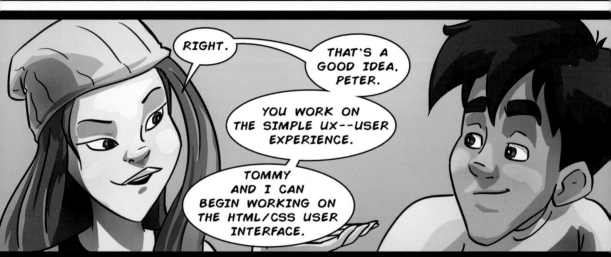

RIGHT.

THAT'S A GOOD IDEA, PETER.

YOU WORK ON THE SIMPLE UX--USER EXPERIENCE.

TOMMY AND I CAN BEGIN WORKING ON THE HTML/CSS USER INTERFACE.

YES.

THAT'S THE UI, OR USER INTERFACE.

BASED OFF PETER'S SITE MAP, I'LL CREATE SIMPLE GRAPHICS.

AFTER YOU GET STARTED WITH THE HTML/CSS, YOU CAN USE MY GRAPHICS WITH THE CODE.

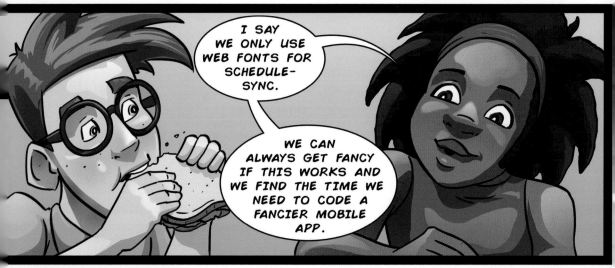

HEY POWER CODERS.

MS. JONES TOLD ME WHAT YOU WERE ALL UP TO, SO I WANTED TO COME LEARN ABOUT SCHEDULE-SYNC FOR MYSELF.

LOOKS INTERESTING!

THANKS, PRINCIPAL GORDON.

I LOVE THE SCHEDULE-SYNC SITE MAP, PETER.

SIMPLE AND EASY TO UNDERSTAND.

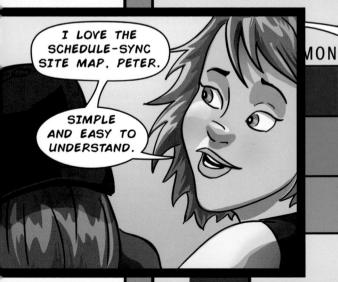

SCHEDULE - SYNC

MON

THE COLOR CODING FOR EACH OF US WAS NAYA'S IDEA.

WED

SHE TEXTED ME SOME DESIGNS, AND I SIMPLIFIED IT FOR THE SITE MAP FOR NOW.

I CAME UP WITH A SCHEDULE-SYNC LOGO, TOO.

GRACE AND I ALREADY STARTED CODING WITH HTML/CSS.

```
<div class="cd-schedule cd-schedule--loading          margin-bottom-l
  <div class="cd-schedule__timeline">
    <ul>
      <li><span>09:00</span></li>
      <li><span>09:30</span></li>
      <!-- additional elements here -->
    </ul>
  </div> <!-- .cd-schedule__timeline -->

  <div class="cd-schedule__events">
    <ul>
      <li class="cd-schedule__group">
        <div class="cd-schedule__top-info">          ></div>

        <ul>
          <li class="cd-schedule__event">
            <a data-start="09:30" data-end="10:30"  da         ="event-abs
              <em class="cd-schedule_name">Abs Ci
            </a>
          </li>


          <!-- other events here -->

      </li>

      <li class="cd-schedule__group">
        <div class="cd-schedule__top-info"><span
```

I'M USING HTML 5 NOW.

IT'S THE MOST RECENT VERSION OF HTML, WHICH ALSO MAKES USE OF CSS.

CSS STANDS FOR "CASCADING STYLE SHEETS."

IT MAKES IT EASY TO CREATE UNIFORM WEBPAGES BECAUSE IT ALLOWS THINGS LIKE FONT STYLES AND TABLE SIZES TO BE DEFINED AND CODED ONCE FOR SEVERAL PAGES, RATHER THAN CODING THEM IN HTML AGAIN AND AGAIN.

HOLD ON.

I'LL TEXT ALEXIS BOYD AND ASK HER FOR SOME ADVICE.

WOW!

YOU HAVE THE PHONE NUMBER OF THE CEO OF YOGA-YOGURT?

THAT'S EPIC!

ALEXIS BOYD TEXTED BACK.

SHE SUGGESTS WE TAKE THE HARD DRIVE OVER TO A DATA RECOVERY SERVICE CALLED DATA DEN.

IT'S NOT FAR FROM HERE.

A DATA RECOVERY SPECIALIST NAMED LANCE OWNS IT. HE MIGHT BE ABLE TO HELP US.

I HOPE WE CAN GET OUR CODE BACK.

THAT'S THE LAST TIME I'LL WORK OFF AN EXTERNAL HARD DRIVE WITHOUT MAKING BACKUPS OF MY CODE.

AGREED.

LESSON LEARNED.

DON'T LOSE THAT DRIVE.

23

HI.

WELCOME TO DATA DEN. I'M LANCE.

HOW CAN I HELP YOU?

HI, LANCE.

WE HAVE A PORTABLE HARD DRIVE WE CAN'T ACCESS!

AND WE REALLY NEED THE CODE OFF IT.

ALEXIS BOYD RECOMMENDED YOU AND DATA DEN.

SHE SAID YOU MIGHT BE ABLE TO RECOVER OUR CODE.

YOU KNOW ALEXIS BOYD?

I MET HER AT THE ENTREPRENEURS CLUB MEETING AT MY SCHOOL.

SHE HELPED US GET OUR BUSINESS IDEA FOR OUR SCHEDULING APP. SCHEDULE-SYNC.

BUT WE NEED TO GET IT UP AND RUNNING SOON SO WE CAN FIND TIME TO WORK ON IT MORE THIS SUMMER.

WE HAVE IMPORTANT HTML AND CSS CODE ON HERE FOR THE WEB APP.

THE FILES WE NEED ARE SCHEDULESYNC.HTML AND A FOLDER CALLED SCHEDULESYNC_ASSETS.

25

DO YOU HAVE ANY IDEA HOW LONG IT MIGHT BE?

WE'RE PRESSED FOR TIME.

WE NEED TO GET THIS PROJECT FINISHED BEFORE SCHOOL ENDS LATER THIS WEEK.

RIGHT.

WE COULD EVEN LET YOU BE A PART OF OUR BUSINESS IN EXCHANGE FOR YOUR RECOVERY SERVICES.

NO NEED.

I'LL GLADLY DO IT FOR FREE.

I OWE ALEXIS BOYD A FAVOR ANYWAY.

AND I LOOK AT DATA RECOVERY AS A PUZZLE I WORK TO SOLVE.

I'M IN BUSINESS HERE, YES, BUT IT'S NOT THE MONEY THAT DRIVES ME, IT'S THE INTELLECTUAL CHALLENGE.

THANKS.

WE APPRECIATE THIS.

I LOVE TO DISMANTLE THESE DEVICES AND GET AT THE DATA THAT'S HIDING IN THERE.

26

A FEW DAYS LATER

DATA DEN
DATA RECOVERY

NEWTON BANK

THANKS FOR COMING BY SO QUICKLY.

AFTER I GOT YOUR TEXT EARLIER WITH THE GOOD NEWS, WE DECIDED TO COME HERE AS SOON AS SCHOOL WAS OVER.

YES, I WAS ABLE TO COMPLETELY RECOVER YOUR CODE.

YOUR HTML/CSS IS VERY IMPRESSIVE, BY THE WAY.

THANK YOU SO MUCH. YOU SAVED US FROM DISASTER!

YES, THANKS!

WHAT WAS THE PROBLEM?

IT TURNS OUT THAT THE USB PORT ON THE DRIVE ITSELF HAD A BAD CONNECTION.

THE DRIVE ITSELF IS FINE.

I SOLDERED THE CONNECTION AND THE DRIVE IS WORKING AGAIN.

SUMMER

THE HTML/CSS SCHEDULE-SYNC WEB APP WORKS GREAT!

IT LOOKS GREAT, TOO, THANKS TO NAYA'S AWESOME DESIGN.

I CAN SEE THE MONEY-MAKING POTENTIAL OF SCHEDULE-SYNC ALREADY.

THANKS.

	MON	TUES	WED	THURS	FRI	SAT	SUN
PETER							
NAYA							
TOMMY							
GRACE							

WORKING ON THE CLOUD NOW MAKES IT EASY FOR US TO ALL ACCESS THE FILES REMOTELY.

WE CAN ALL WORK ON SCHEDULE-SYNC ALL SUMMER.

LANCE'S IDEA TO WORK WITH OUR FILES IN THE CLOUD HAS SAVED US EVEN MORE TIME.

AND ACCORDING TO SCHEDULE-SYNC, NEXT WEEK WE'LL HAVE THREE FULL DAYS WHEN NONE OF US ARE WORKING.

THAT'S GREAT NEWS!

NOW WE CAN GET TOGETHER TO KEEP IMPROVING SCHEDULE-SYNC SO WE CAN HAVE A BEST-SELLING APP THAT WILL MAKE US RICH!

MAKING MONEY WOULD BE NICE.

WE CAN ALSO USE THE FREE TIME TO RELAX.